On the other s

I remind the promise.

Beyond the walls... Someone is always there.

After Six o'Clock

~Nightfall~

Horror Short Story Tetralogy

ELENA CARTER, DANIEL ENRIQUEZ,

THERESA JACOBS & LUCY LOMBOS

This is a Horror Short Story Tetralogy,
published by Lombosco Publications, Canada.

Date Published: August 6, 2020

Dedication

To our beloved families

who always support and accompany us in our writing

journeys.

But sorry for frightening you, guys in this tetralogy.

- Elena, Daniel, Theresa and Lucy

Table of Contents

Introduction #1

As two bored teenagers on a Halloween night decide to take a peek into their future using a mirror portal, something goes terribly wrong and the innocent game turns into their worst nightmare. "Mirror, Mirror on the Wall" is a chill and a thrill.

- Elena Carter,
Fantasy Writer,
Varna, Bulgaria

Introduction #2

When I was young, I loved to listen to my grandmother's horror tales. At my age now, I would like to pass on to the new generation one of the stories that I remembered so well.

"The Immunity" is my grandmother's original story. However, I followed the important elements of horror. Hence, this is an account written with creative imagination, fear, surprise, and mystery. Aside from those elements, it was written with a special kind of writing style, primarily to know its real message and the foreshadowed traits for one's learning and enjoyment.

I am the proud grandson of the family's storyteller and her subject who was my great grandfather. I learned from them valuable traits such as faith, sharp thinking, decisiveness, courage, and strength of character and morals.

- Daniel Enriquez

Marine Biologist,

Former Councilor of Puerto Galera for 12 Consecutive Years,

Author of several Municipal Ordinances,

Puerto Galera, Or. Mindoro, Philippines

Introduction #3

When we think of ghosts, our minds tend to the most common theme, a haunted house- generally, the spirits of previous tenants who perhaps died long-ago. Or of tragedy, murders, suicides, children lost to fires. But what if there was a room, a simple, small, unassuming room, only this room was more than what it seemed? What if it was the limbo between worlds? And what if whatever was in that room wanted out?

- Theresa Jacobs,

Author of Paranormal, Horror, Suspense Books, (Speculative Fiction), Children's Books, and Poetry

https://theresajcbs.wixsite.com/authorpage

Toronto, Canada

Introduction #4

The idea to launch a horror short story tetralogy was hatched on May 31, 2020, at 3:00 pm. I sent a message to Ms. Theresa Jacobs, a Canadian paranormal/horror author of several books, to solicit her contribution on this writing project. Her response was awesome! She assured me of her genuine support. Then, I talked to Mr. Daniel Enriquez from the Philippines. He agreed to pen a beautiful story as well. Aside from them, I invited Ms. Elena Carter from Bulgaria, a fantasy writer herself, to try her hand in this kind of genre. It was pure joy and excitement to know that each one of us will write a horror tale.

Since everybody had to stay home due to the unprecedented pandemic, I became engrossed with an online course from a prestigious university in the US, no less. Amidst a busy schedule full of readings and requirements, I had my inspiration. On June 3, 2020, I began writing my story, "Timelessness".

I hope that both young and old readers will find my special book offer compelling. It will provide them a vivid picture of a new kind of a fiction. This tale will give them some goose-bump moments and educate them at the same time. It shares traces of history and culture. It also attempts to shape a new understanding of the past to the contemporary world. Moreover, it is value-laden because they can learn the traits of courage, faith, and love. "Timelessness" is worth-reading and believing.

- Lucy Lombos

Academy Directress and Language and Literacy Teacher,
http://lomboscoacademy.com/senior-incorporators/,
Author of Children's Books, YA Novel, Biographies and Fables
www.lucylombos.com
British Columbia, Canada

On the other side of the mirror...

Mirror, Mirror on the Wall

By Elena Carter

"I'm not sure about this!" Mallory looked around the room nervously.

"Come on, it's gonna be fun! Don't be such a chicken!" Courtney was rushing around the room, her hands full of candles, but she was looking for more.

"I read that scrying can be dangerous," Mallory insisted.

"Well, you know what, life is dangerous. It leads to death. Proven fact," Courtney said while adjusting the mirrors. "Would you pass me that candleholder?"

"Isn't that too many candles? I thought there should be one," Mallory said. "Two mirrors, facing each other, one candle between them."

"Bo-ring..." Courtney rolled her eyes. "The more, the better, I'm sure. Plus, we're creating the right atmosphere! Come on, stop being so negative! Better think of a question you're gonna ask!"

"I don't know... what did you come up with? Gonna ask about Alex? If he's the one? That's what that article said, you know. That in this tunnel of reflections, you will see the love of your life, your destined mate..."

"I'm sure Alex isn't the one. But I am going to ask who it is. Imagine if we see someone we know!"

"I don't know if we're gonna see anyone at all and I kinda hope we don't. It's a bit creepy," Mallory shrugged. "I'm really not sure about this."

"It's supposed to be. That's what Halloween is for! Look, can we just have some fun? I was so happy when we came up with this idea, I really can't stand the thought of spending another Halloween evening watching Addams Family with my Mom!" Courtney sat on the bed, with her legs crossed and with a pleading look in her eyes.

"All right," Mallory surrendered with a smile. "Let's do it. I am a bit scared, but I guess that's the idea, anyway!"

"Finally!" Courtney's face lit up with a big grin. "Got the matches? Let's light the candles first and then switch the light off."

"You might wanna close the window, too," Mallory suggested.

Courtney followed her friend's advice. The girls lit all the candles they'd prepared for the ritual and placed them around the two mirrors, which were facing each other.

"Ok, here we go…" Courtney looked at the scene and nodded approvingly. "Now… kill the lights!"

Mallory let out a nervous giggle and hit the switch on the wall.

With the room lit only by a dozen candles, the atmosphere changed drastically within a second.

Mallory slowly moved closer to Courtney, who was standing by the mirrors. She couldn't make herself look in the mirror. In fact, she tried to avoid looking in that direction at all.

Courtney, on the other hand, looked absolutely fascinated. She grabbed a chair from the desk and positioned it as close to the mirrors as she could. She then sat down on it; while looking into the tunnel of reflections, lit only by the candles' dancing flames.

"So... What do we do?" Mallory was obviously feeling very uncomfortable. She made herself walk over to the bed, though, past the mirrors, and sat down on the edge of the bed. "You wanna go first? Gonna ask your question?"

"I don't know... Should I say it out loud?" Courtney giggled. "Mirror, mirror on the wall..."

The light of one of the candles, the closest one to the mirror, suddenly went out.

"Crap. Where are the matches?"

"You had them!" Mallory was becoming even more nervous.

"Oh yeah, that's right, here they are. There we go."

Courtney lit the candle again and sighed.

"Ok, where were we... I want to see who my other

half is!"

Courtney leaned over to the mirrors. Silence filled the room. Mallory could hear her own heartbeat somewhere in the area of her throat. For some reason, she didn't even want to move.

The girls sat there silently for a few minutes when Courtney suddenly screamed: "I saw something!"

Mallory jumped.

"God, you scared me! What did you see?"

"I don't know. I'm not sure. Some movement. Like a shadow. Come have a look!"

"I'll pass, thank you," Mallory giggled nervously. "I'm just fine where I am."

"Come on! You're missing everything! There! I saw it again!" Courtney was leaning in closer.

"Are you sure it's a good idea to lean that close? And are you sure it's not your own shadow when you sit like that, practically in between the mirrors?" Mallory asked.

"It's not! I can't even see my reflection! See?"

Courtney waved her hand in front of the mirror.

"What the hell do you mean??? Courtney?"

"Shit!" Courtney pulled back. "I can't see my reflection! I just realized! What the hell?!"

"Courtney, you're scaring me. Let's stop this, please!" Mallory was almost screaming. "I'm turning the light on!"

"No, wait! There has to be an explanation!" Courtney reached out again, and this time touched the mirror.

"Don't!" Mallory screamed.

"Mal, would you snap out of it already? I' m'--" Courtney stopped in the middle of the phrase. "Mal? I think I'm stuck." Now she sounded scared.

"What the hell do you mean you're stuck? Is that a stupid joke?" Mallory jumped up and headed towards the switch. "I've had enough of this!"

"Mal, help! Please!!!" Courtney begged.

Mallory hit the switch on the wall, but nothing happened.

"Shit!!!"

She tried again and again.

"Mal, help me!!! I'm serious!"

"Courtney, the light isn't working! What's happening?" Mallory was about to cry. She looked at her friend. Courtney was sitting in a funny position, the palm of her hand touching the mirror's surface. Her neck turned towards Mallory as if she was not only asking for help but also terrified of looking at her hand.

Mallory made a couple steps towards her. She finally forced herself to look in the mirror.

There was no reflection of Courtney's hand. In fact, her hand was already inside the mirror, as if the shiny surface was liquid, and she had dipped her fingers into it.

She looked at Courtney's face and saw her eyes full of fear, lips trembling, tears running down her cheeks.

"Mal..." Courtney whispered. "I'm so scared. Please help me..."

"It's ok. Everything's gonna be ok." Mallory took a

couple of steps towards Courtney. Each step took a huge effort as her body was almost paralyzed with fear. "We'll get you out of there, don't worry."

A sudden gust of wind opened the window and blew out half of the candles. Both girls screamed.

When Mallory looked back at Courtney, she saw that half of her arm was already inside the mirror.

"Oh, my God! Courtney!" Mallory burst into tears. She gathered whatever courage she had, ran over to her friend, grabbing her other arm and trying to pull her away from the mirror. The chair Courtney was sitting on, fell. Both girls ended up on the floor, and for a moment, Mallory let go of her arm.

"Girls, what's going on? I heard you screaming!"

As Courtney's mother opened the door abruptly, the draft blew out the rest of the candles in a split second.

"NO!!!" Mallory heard herself scream. At first, she didn't even recognize her own voice, masked by the sound of breaking glass. A second later, she realized that it was also the only voice she heard. Courtney didn't make a sound.

"Why is it so dark here?" Courtney's mother reached for the switch which this time obeyed instantly, and the light came on.

Mallory was sitting on the floor, in tears, surrounded by hundreds of shining shards. One of the mirrors was smashed, the other one was whole, but it wasn't a mirror anymore. Its surface was a dull grey and didn't reflect anything.

As Mallory was gasping for air, she realized that there was no sign of Courtney in the room. All that was left of her best friend was her golden locket pendant hanging off the corner of what used to be a mirror.

I remind the promise.

The Immunity

* * * * * * * * * * *

By Daniel Enriquez

"My father hooked his hands on one of the roots of the Mangrove Tree," my grandmother recalled the wrestling scene of my great grandfather versus his enemy.

My grandmother's real name was Regina, meaning Queen in Spanish; and in the Filipino language, "lola" is the equivalent of grandmother. Regina's nickname was "Inang". So, the whole family and I fondly called her Lola Inang with respect, endearment and love.

My great grandfather was called Lolo Higino. Based on my lola's stories, Lolo Higino had a little bit of Spanish blood. He was born during the time when the Spaniards colonized the Philippines. The stories went

18

on to say that my great grandfather's name became synonymous to quickness of the mind. For some reason, he was known to have possessed a great sense of maturity, resilience and the ability to be successful in anything he would undertake.

"I could imagine how intense and ferocious the fight was! Who won, Lola Inang?" I asked.

Lola Inang was a clever and holy woman. The lines on her face were visible, but she was clearly a beauty. She was already sixty-five years old when she was narrating the story to me. She did not answer my question right away. Instead, she first recollected, "The Mangrove tree brought the memories of my father, your courageous great grandfather."

"Probably that's the reason why I'm fond of those tropical trees that grow above the ground and on salty shores. I learned from the school that they can also survive on fresh water conditions," I said and continued as smart as I could, "They naturally grow at the coastal, inter tidal zone. It's peculiar that they flourish on a beach area, flooded during high tide and no water during low tide. But of course, I learned many things from you, Lola."

"That's the wonder of Science!" Lola Inang remarked, seemingly she liked Science, too. She further said, "You are correct! They grow naturally on the tidal shores. However, these past three decades, humans started to plant Mangroves after realizing their importance in the ecosystem."

"Lola, Mangrove trees looked fascinating to me because of their very strong twisted roots," I said just like a primary grade school boy's attentiveness to listen to storytelling.

"That's right! Their extensive, stilt root systems shelter small fishes and provide a lot of useful things both to marine animals and humans; also to our environment."

I paused to take everything in. "Lola, the significance of the Mangroves to you is still about Lolo Higino's story, right?"

She also paused and changed her mood.

"I always wonder about the grueling fight at the coastal area," I told her.

"Your Lolo Higino defeated the evil spirit," Lola Inang

this time, replied to me with fear and yet with accompanying great pride.

"Was that Aswang?" I asked. Actually, the mere word gave me a scare.

"Yes, Aswang! For the Filipinos, it was a ghoulish creature. At times, they can look like animals, weird human or forms of nature. Very mysterious!" Lola Inang continued. "This hairy Aswang's goal is survival. His kind is searching for food, particularly human's liver. He would grab anyone to eat."

My grandmother stood up to look out the half-closed window. Her face was pensive, as if looking at the scenario right in front of her. Like a spectator in an arena, I closely watched too, as the story unraveled.

The fight between Lolo Higino and Aswang occurred and started at the intersection of Lazareto and the famous Calapan Pier.

Lolo Higino was a coachman. Kutsero, in Filipino. He had a calesa or a karatela, a coach drawn by a horse.

It was his job to transport passengers to and from the busy Pier. From Lazareto, he drove his calesa to

Salong, bound for Calapan Pier. This was his usual route. Salong was one, small village of the Municipality of Calapan in the province of Oriental Mindoro.

"I will not forget that very spot. That intersection was where the horrific fight between the forces of evil versus a good, strong, determined human took place." Lola Inang's voice was almost a whisper.

While on the calesa, Lolo Higino felt moisture on his nape. It felt exactly like a cold breath of somebody very close to his body.

He knew that very moment that something enigmatic was bound to happen.

"Pater Noster, qui es...." his voice trembled as he started to utter the Our Father in Latin. "Qui....es qui." He mustered enough strength to continue praying, with the words unwilling to roll out. "Pater Noster qui es in coelis." He groped, but was successful this time.

"Pater Noster qui es in coelis!" This time more emphatic. "Sanctificetur nomen tuum." He went on reverent, yet loud and confident. Despite his throat dried and his hair drenched with sweat out of fear, he was able to finish the prayer.

He was right, after all. When he turned around, he saw a big, black dog with huge fangs. His eyes were bloodshot, the big ears were erected. It tried to come extremely close, its sharp and pointed teeth ready to eat its human prey.

Lola Inang stopped. My curiosity lingered. "What happened next, Lola?" The stillness in the room was too much. As the story continued, we both ignored it, but the fear was enveloping us. There were goosebumps all over my arms.

"The wild dog changed into a monstrous being," she said and both of us lay in bed.

The narration proceeded. I listened with so much eagerness and I kept everything in my mind...

Aswang grabbed Lolo Higino on his nape. He dragged him to a hidden place where he could kill, chop, and feast on him. Lola Inang repeated that the human liver was Aswang's favorite food.

Lolo Higino realized that he was being dragged to the sea. Actually, the evil creature wanted to bring him to the Mangrove area, and he did. The area had a massive collection of Mangroves at the base of the mountain. This was the marshy side of the Pier.

To say that he was scared was an understatement. He could feel it all over his being. But he knew he could not lose hope. With all his might, he tried to reach and extend his hand. He was able to grip on one of the sturdy roots of the Mangrove tree.

Lolo Higino knew he had to give a good fight. What weapon could he use? He opened his mouth and took a huge bite on the right ankle of Aswang.

The grisly creature became furious. The pain was tremendous. His ankle was his body's weakest part. The teeth of Lolo Higino went through the skin and went deep... so profound that caused a lot of blood. Part of the muscle was being mangled. The evil one's scream meant that he was in severe anguish, and he begged for mercy.

I covered my ears. I almost heard the scary sound from Aswang. Lola Inang looked at me. "Do you want to continue?" I simply nodded my head.

Aswang's eyes locked with the bold man. For the second time, it was a look begging for mercy. It was a cry for help, pleading for him to be released. To be free from pain.

Despite his emotions overcoming him, Lolo Higino made sure he sounded forceful, "Do you promise not to bother me anymore, including my family?"

Aswang seemed to have understood the man's words. His head bowed, his shoulders crunched, and without any doubt, he was saying yes.

"Are you sure? Say it aloud!" In his powerful thought, Lolo Higino demanded, as he deepened his bite to Aswang's ankle.

Aswang's glare changed from anger to pain. It showed only defeat and submission. His movement gave his message. "Yes, I will never ever touch you again and your children's children. And the rest of the family."

"A promise should never be broken," Lola Inang recounted what Lolo Higino told Aswang, and she added, "Aswang agreed not to bother all of us. With that, your Lolo released him."

"You mean all of us have that immunity?" I asked Lola Inang.

"I believe that the promise holds."

"Are we really protected?" I asked again for assurance.

"Hopefully, you are untouchable forever!" Lola Inang ended her storytelling. I saw her body relaxed as well.

"I have to memorize Pater Noster."

"Yes, my boy. It will save you. But any prayer from the heart is as strong as any fervent prayer."

"Wherever you are, Aswang... I am the great-grandson of Lolo Higino! Remember your promise!"

The wind blew in response. I felt Aswang's cold and creepy breath on my nape.

"Hmmm, I hope it's his pledge to me and to the entire clan," I uttered with so much faith to what my Lolo Higino and Lola Inang defended and believed all throughout those years.

After that, my Lola Inang taught me the Lord's Prayer in Latin.

"Pater noster, qui es in coelis," I started to utter the

prayer. Its graceful rhythm lulled me to sleep.

Beyond the walls...

The Room

By Theresa Jacobs

"Did you get your bed set up okay?"

Melanie looked up from her iPhone and rolled her eyes as she sat on her perfectly made bed.

"I know the move was tough, so try to get some rest." He turned to go, paused and said, "I love you, Mel." He blinked back a tear closing his daughter's door; she had not said a word.

Skirting the piled boxes, he stopped in the spare room. The small room had no windows, and he flipped on the light. The walls had been painted a deep brown with a single bare bulb dangling from the ceiling. Two steps to the center of the room and the door whisked shut with a click. Jackson's heart gave a stutter at the sound, and as he looked over his shoulder, the light

29

went out.

He blinked at the complete blackness and did an about face towards the door. Only two steps later, he could not find the door or a wall. He waved his hands around and shuffled forward.

"Hello?" he called, unsure why. Okay, stay calm. Just go straight and find a wall. He walked forward, arms up, hands out, and still nothing. "Come on!" He walked quicker, expecting to ram palms first into a solid wall. His heart thumped. "MELANIE!" he shouted and his voice did not resound, it came out muffled, like yelling into a pillow.

A feather-light touch brushed his forearm. Goosebumps prickled his flesh. He stood stock still, crossing his arms over his chest. Then the voices came. They whispered unintelligibly, some close to his ear, others from a great distance. Things brushed past him, the air whirled, wispy tendrils caressed his arms, his face, and pressed harder against his legs.

"Who's there?" He spun in blindness. "Hello?" A cold sweat broke out on his brow.

Unseen icy fingers continued to brush at his flesh.

His skin crawled. He stumbled forward, then left, then right. He turned in circles and called out again. After hours of darkness and fear, he curled into a fetal position on the floor and covered his head.

·····•••●●●●•••····

"Are you getting up?"

Jackson squinted at the bright light and the dark silhouette in the doorway. It clicked in his brain. The door is open, get out.

"Mel…" he croaked, his voice hoarse. She turned and walked away. Panicked that the door would close again, he pushed his sore body up off the floor and stumbled out of the room. Only then did he notice that he'd wet himself.

"Melanie?" He tried again, but it was too late; the front door slammed shut. Looking over his shoulder, he saw the spare room door was shut.

He knew he didn't have time to think about last night and rushed to the bathroom. Embarrassed by the state he was in, he threw his jeans into the trash and took a quick shower before racing off to his first day at the new job.

"Mel, I'm home," he called, entering the house. There was no response. He walked through the kitchen and gave a gentle rap on her door. "Honey? You didn't…" Her room was empty.

He texted her: where r u?

Jackson moved nervously to the spare room. The door was still shut, and he dare not open it. Tearing open the bag he'd picked up from the hardware store, he pulled out a latch, a screwdriver, and a padlock. Fifteen minutes later, he clicked the padlock into place, tucking the key away in his pocket. Realizing that he still had not heard from Melanie, he checked his phone. It was six-thirty. He couldn't eat, and he didn't want to watch tv; all he could do was worry. A few hours later, he decided to go lay on her bed, and as he entered the hall, the lock on the spare room caught his eye.

"No! She wouldn't go in there. But what if?" Heart racing, he fumbled the key from his pocket. He closed his eyes as the lock snapped open. Fingers gripped vise-like to the door frame; he turned the knob. The door opened to the black room, the rectangle of light stretching his shadow to the opposite wall. He reached in and flipped the switch. The room lit up, empty.

"Oh, thank God." He released the breath he didn't know he was holding, and as his foot crested the threshold, a voice cried out from nothingness.

"Daddy!"

"Melanie?" He yelled out, scooting back from the open door. "Melanie?"

No response came.

"What am I going to do?" He tapped his forehead, squeezing his eyes shut. What came to his mind was the old movie, Poltergeist. "I need a rope!" He jumped up and ran to the heap of boxes in the living room. Tossing them aside, careless of contents, reading labels. He tore into one marked 'basement junk' and found a long orange extension cord.

"I'm coming, baby!"

Turning the corner to the hall, Jackson saw the door was again closed. Shivers raced up his spine. His footsteps faltered. That's when it hit him to get a flashlight, a weapon, and something to block the door from closing.

Ten minutes later, Jackson had the extension cord strung through his belt loops and tied off. Six of the heaviest boxes he could find pressed against the now opened door. A butcher knife in one hand and a flashlight in the other. He walked weak-kneed to the center of the room. "Melanie?" he whispered, and the lights went out.

Looking over his shoulder, he could see the square of light cast from the open door, yet it didn't penetrate the inky dark. He clicked on the flashlight and found the same results. The brightness haloed the casing, but no further. He gripped the knife tighter.

"Mel?" he whispered, and something touched his arm. He jolted away, and a soft breeze caressed his neck. Shivers raced down his spine, and his guts knotted. He aimed the feeble light up near his face. "Who's there?" he whispered.

"Daddy!"

"Melanie? Where are you, baby?"

A woman wept in the distance; fingers reached out of the blackness, touching him everywhere. Jackson cringed but could not escape the hands. They brushed his cheeks, pulled at his sleeves and clawed at his legs. Remembering the knife in his hand, he swiped the air blindly. His skin tightened at the constant caresses; it was like walking through cobwebs knowing they were full of spiders.

"MELANIE, ANSWER ME!" he screamed into the abyss.

A flicker of bluish light angled from above, giving sight to the room. The darkness was filled with ghouls. Faces with empty eye sockets, elongated-toothless mouths. Their skin like granite and their hands were seeking egress. It was them touching him, their cries reaching his ears, and their coldness leeching his heat.

He dropped the ineffectual knife, drew his arms back into his sides, and closed his eyes. Jackson moved his fingers to the electrical cord around his waist and gripped it for dear life. "I'm sorry, baby," he mumbled as tears fell from his eyes.

"Help me, daddy!"

He could not leave her. Turning back, he opened his eyes and waited. When the blue light flashed again, he began to count. He removed the cord from his belt and tied it as best he could around the flashlight, then dropped it to the floor. He did not want to think about what would happen if, two feet from the light, he could no longer see it.

At twenty, he ran.

"Now!" he called, his arms out, praying to catch his daughter and not someone else. As the incandescent glow gave him vision again, he angled left, wrapping his arms around Melanie's ice-cold body. He spun them quickly to face—he hoped—the direction from which he came and waited.

All around them, the voices wept, screamed, moaned and spoke in tongues. High-pitched squeals, or low, angry growls assaulted their ears. Fingers pressed into their flesh and pulled at their hair and clothes. Melanie sobbed openly; her face buried hard into his chest.

The room flicked into sight again, the pale, eyeless faces and slack mouths pressed closer. Their hunger for life clear in their seeking hands. The melanoid space held hundreds of these wanton creatures and Jackson decided it would not have them. He spotted the circle of light on the floor and swept his daughter into his arms.

He ran. In one fast motion, he scooped up the flashlight and with it, the lifeline out of Hell.

Once he passed a certain point, the sky stopped illuminating, and he could see the square opening at the doorway. The moaning from the inky black sounded distant but rose in a crescendo as though the spirits knew they were losing their guests. A cruel, icy wind rose. He pressed on, fighting the forces, and the fingers dropped away from his legs. He stumbled through the door, falling on top of Melanie in the hallway. Not wasting a second, he turned, pushed the boxes away from the door and secured the deadbolt.

Melanie's eyes were closed, her breathing was shallow. He scooped her back into his arms, walked into the kitchen and turned on the gas burner. Her eyes opened, and he said. "We're going home, baby."

★ ★

Someone is always there.

Timelessness

By Lucy Lombos

"Barbakal lives forever," my grandma said.

In my innocent mind, I knew him.

"Boom! Bang! Bang!"

I heard the loud sounds. Night after night, they seemed to come from ammunitions that disturbed my beloved Philippines. As a matter of fact, they kept ringing in my mind. My grandmother passed on to me the historic portrait of the war. Everything was tainted with blood. The noise was distressing. I absorbed all even the untold images.

The frequent sounds of the bombings and the killings of the oppressed folks were heard once again; so powerful that they all flashed in my consciousness…

well, as in so many times that rattled me. The echo of the story made me a part of the occurrence of the dreadful saga. History would repeat time after time.

Then it began. "Awooo... Awooo!"

The frightful dogs howled for so long. The creepy silence of the night agitated them.

"Oh grandma, I'm so scared," I screamed. I ran to grandma. Then I grabbed her shawl. I felt safe when I covered myself with it.

"Awooo... Awooo!"

The wild dogs continued to groan as if all of them were in excruciating pain. The bats flew and hovered up the gloomy sky, at the time when the stars seemed to hide. The stars that should decorate the night sky with brilliance disappeared. Instead, a blank page took its place, joined by an unseen shadow of an evil presence. The moon looked somewhat round, yet it gave a sallow light. It manifested a macabre scene. I felt almost sick, and I sensed the eeriness of the night that penetrated into my physical body.

"Barbakal lives forever," my grandma rehashed.

My grandma was seventy years old, but her mind was still sharp. She had long hair, wrinkled face, and skinny body with a height of an average Filipina. Her stature looked holy because she acquired the steadfast faith in God, a trait that I witnessed and learned from her.

"Is there a super typhoon?" I asked grandma. The rain poured like a tempest. The wind blew in gusts. It accompanied the devastating pitter-patter of the rain and the dogs' wails.

"I think so," she replied.

All of a sudden, the lights went off. Straightaway, I saw a silhouette appeared at the wall in the living room.

"We lost power again?" I asked her while my hair started to stand. Then, I tried to ignore what I saw. Well, it could be the Acacia tree outside, swaying due to the strong typhoon.

I could feel our nipa hut's bamboo flooring turned icy cold, and it creaked in a quiet vibration. I knew that if I would choose to look down, I could probably see a ghost. I would rather not look. I would not peep down. I imagined ghastly thoughts.

"Where's our lamp?" grandma asked.

"I couldn't find it either, grandma," I replied while I started to feel the chill sensation. I could hear the icy, suffering voice. I followed my grandma wherever she went around our hut to check and secure everything.

"Fine… Likewise, this circumstance that we're in already happened in the past during storm surges. The mornings turned into nights too soon. The intense storms took us by surprise. Well, we can use the candle at the altar. After the Angelus and dinner, we will just lie down; I will tell you a story," she promised; such a promise that I would look forward to.

For a few times, I peeped out the window and looked up the sky. The sun veiled itself. It was so swift and noiseless. Its powerful glow faded away in haste, as if it did not show up in the morning. My grandma would say that it looked like the quick death of the sun. Ah, so many thoughts came into my mind! But the nightfall brought about an inescapable darkness and strangeness to me.

The torrential raindrops played like an orchestra that night. Joining the symphony were lightning blasts and roars of thunder. Yet, their blaring sound began to be the center of our attention and wariness. For this reason, the moon fully hid itself as well. Hence, it did not provide us the illumination that we needed. Oh, I distracted myself on what I was really feeling!

Our ancestral pendulum clock gave out a resounding chime, prompting all corners of the hut that it was six o'clock. I blinked my eyes hard to make sure of what I saw. I was pretty sure that it was fifteen minutes before the hour. Fifteen minutes before the Angelus. Were my eyes fooling me?

I shook my head, trying to remind myself to be brave. My grandma kept on moving. I got tired, and I rested on the sofa. That moment, I was waiting for her near the altar that was placed at the center of our hut.

Without delay, grandma lit the candle. She arranged the flowers at the altar. Both of us knelt down.

"The angel of the Lord declared unto Mary", grandma led the prayer on top of her voice even though we were just the two of us.

"And she conceived by the Holy Spirit," I responded. I also made my voice louder, more alert than before. I believed the prayer could ward off evil spirits.

We finished the Angelus. That was a habitual exercise of the religious piety in our clan. Right after the prayer, we had a simple dinner.

Afterwards, I was swift in washing the dishes. I dried them and returned them all to the cabinet. I didn't like to be left alone at the kitchen, especially during brownouts and super typhoons.

In that particular moment, I couldn't control my thoughts. I could see distorted images on the frames that grandma had hung on our wall a long time ago. Those were the pictures of my parents who already went to the bosom of our Creator.

"Awooo… Awooo!"

The massive dogs ululated in Ilang. Their cries would be heard at nightfall, even on rainy season.

We lived in Ilang, a remote and creepy wilderness beyond the main village where an old church was still erected. Houses were far apart with the gap almost a hundred meters. Folks wore hats. Men carried along their bolos which were their sharp tools and protective weapons against danger or violence caused by deranged neighbors, insane attackers and evil spirits.

The roads in Ilang lined many trees and varied flowers in constant bloom.

The coprahan was far away from us. It was the place where the coconuts were peeled and cleaned. It was situated at the end of Ilang. Grandma worked there long before I was born.

I recalled that it was at coprahan where I heard the full story of the Japanese invasion. Even though I was only eight years old, my grandma's narrative account of the war and what happened to the Filipino soldiers remained in my absorbent mind.

Four years after, I welcomed anew grandma's recount of the war. She would never get tired re-telling me of that horrific story. I, too, was interested to listen to her story over and over again.

"World War II took place here in our country when Japan invaded us in 1942 to 1945. Being located at the Far East, we were the important military target of Japan. The war became known as the Japanese Occupation," my grandma started narrating.

"Grandma, I thought it started in 1941?" I asked her.

"The Japanese launched an attack in our country on December 8, 1941. At that time, we were a territory of the United States."

"So, the prior regime was the US Commonwealth?" I clarified.

"Yes!... The following year, in 1942, the Philippine and American military forces surrendered in Bataan and Corregidor. Then, in 1943, the Japanese declared our country as the Republic of the Philippines. During this World War II, the Filipino soldiers became captives. The Japanese got scared of the strategy of the Americans to retake our country."

"How many Filipinos died in that war?" I asked, imagining the unrelenting maltreatment of the invaders.

"Around half a million!" grandma estimated and went on, "A lot were tortured and executed. Our brave soldiers, including those in guerilla warfare faced the firing squads. One horrible firing squad took place at Cadre, a military camp here in our province."

"But grandma, why was Barbakal known to all of us?"

"He was born here in Mindoro! He became a soldier, deployed at Cadre, who also helped in the guerilla warfare. Manila was an open city at that time. Fighting was intense all over the city. You could see rubbles everywhere. Then, the Japanese had reached our province and maltreated everyone, especially the soldiers who showed fierce aggression."

"And among them was Barbakal, grandma?... What was Barbakal like?"

"Yes!... Barbakal looked robust and gigantic. He was an excellent fighter. His gallantry spread around and reached the imperial Japanese authority.

"How did he fight the imperial Japanese invaders?"

"Well, as a well-trained soldier, he was never afraid in shooting his gun, in attacking the invaders, and in throwing explosives provided by the US military. He also assisted in the guerilla warfare."

"Guerilla?"

"Yeah, they were the armed civilians who helped the Filipino soldiers."

"Let me clear this, Barbakal died in the battle?

"Barbakal, being the tallest soldier, caught the attention of the Japanese military men and officers."

"You mean, the Japanese was amazed of the height of Barbakal?"

"That's right! He was a hulk. But they got mad at him because he was in-charge of providing and distributing the supplies of weaponry and other warfare involvements to the Filipino soldiers. Everything was done in secret as furnished and instructed by the Americans."

"Wow, he was incredible!"

"The Japanese arrested Barbakal. Instead of shooting him at once, they would like to bury him alive.

"Alive? Why did they do that, grandma?"

"I don't know. He was their enemy. Awfully, they prepared his coffin."

"And then what happened?" I was so curious in this part.

"Because Barbakal was too tall and huge for the coffin, the Japanese cut his legs off and laid there at the coffin. Barbakal bled a lot."

"They cut off his legs? Oh, my God!... Did he die right away?"

"Nope!... Please help me!" my grandma imitated Barbakal's lamenting voice.

"It was horrible, grandma! I could feel the pain."

"Please have mercy!" my grandma continued imitating Barbakal's voice. With her normal tone, she proceeded, "Barbakal sought help. But even he cried out aloud, he was buried alive six feet below the ground, much less of his towering height."

"Jesus! That was an unbearable agony!"

"From then on, six o'clock and beyond the time became scary. The people would hear moans and painful cries. They believe that it was him."

The following weekend, the rains continued to pour. The radio shows broadcasted, though, that it ceased to be a super typhoon. And strangely, whenever there would be news about wars and protests in different parts of the world, I couldn't help but think of the story. It kept haunting me.

Barbakal would come back! What kind of war would it be if he returns? A nuclear war? A bio war? For sure, there will be a lot of prolonged wails and yowls.

"Teng!... Teng!... Teng!..." The tintinnabulation of the church bells occurred at six o'clock. So, my grandma and I prayed the Angelus. The sun already set, and the clouds changed its gloomy cast. I could feel that the nature gasped and shed tears, too, as if they were in affliction.

A few minutes later, the jarred dogs began to ululate. The night spread and crept like a poisonous snake on the ground... so deadly. Once more, I heard the painful cries coming from the grave at the farthest end of Ilang. The World War II ended, but Barbakal lives forever.

"Will there be an end to his moaning?" I asked myself. My mind played the question a million times.

One unexpected day, my grandma died of a heart attack. She came home exhausted from work at the coprahan. Her sudden demise saddened me. She was my only treasure.

"Who will take care of me? Who will tell stories to

me?" I sobbed. I would also ask those questions every time her memories crossed my mind. I missed my grandmother particularly at night time when humans fell asleep and while the evil spirits woke up.

"Barbakal lives forever." It lingered in my mind.

But my grandma, who used to say that a lost soul in anguish would seek help, definitely would live forever in the deepest part of my aching heart.

"Oh, dear grandma!" Thinking of her sapped my energy, notably when I was at rest.

My grandma was a great influence in my life. She seemed to have all the answers to my questions. She taught me not to be afraid. Whenever we were at the backyard, she would recite her best-liked quote, "The grass withers and the flowers fall, but the word of our God endures forever."

The next day, the rain stopped. The sun came out like a King in shining armor. At the backyard, I saw and picked the lovely flowers. I offered them at the altar. Thereupon, my grandmother's soft, aged voice whispered her favorite line to my ears.

"Greeting me on such an early morning, grandma?" I asked her.

The flowers swayed. My heart skipped a beat.

"I got it, grandma! Rest in peace."

SPECIAL REQUEST

To all those who bought and read this book-

If you loved this Horror Short Story Tetralogy and have a minute to spare, the author would really appreciate a short review from you to be posted on the site where you bought or read the book. Your help in spreading kind words is a great succor to other readers, especially to the young children from different parts of the world.

GREAT THANKS!

Acknowledgment

We would like to express our deep gratitude to the following people for giving us the big support which we humbly needed in writing this book –

Umberto L. Lombos for publishing this book;

Annie Datu-Enriquez for editing the manuscript;

Jacqueline Leahey
and
Jimmy Belleza

for writing the wonderful blurbs for this tetralogy,

and to our families for giving us the moral support.

We are truly happy and grateful to you all.

Without your generous help, this book may not have been possible.

The Major Sponsors

LOMBOSCO ACADEMY FOUNDATION, INC.

Since 2000

Telephone numbers: 8842-7992; 8842-6519

Address:

11 C. Arellano St/, Phase 1, Katarungan Village, Poblacion, Muntinlupa City, Metro Manila, Philippines

MAGNIFICAN IMMIGRATION AGENCY

https://magnificanimmigration.com/